Best Friends

Best Friends

By K. T. Hao • Illustrated by Giuliano Ferri

TRANSLATED BY ANNIE KUNG

Purple Bear Books

NEW YORK

Ben Bear and Chris Croc are best friends. They run a restaurant together where they serve the most mouthwatering pizzas and luscious desserts in town.

One day, Ben got a new puppy. He named him Luke.

"I'm going to build Luke a doghouse," Ben said to Chris. "Would you give me a hand?"

Chris was glad to help. They sawed and hammered; they painted and decorated. Working together, they built Luke's doghouse in no time at all.

They finished just in time for supper and happily shared one of their mouthwatering pizzas. Then Chris Croc waved good-bye and headed home.

That night Ben Bear could not fall asleep. He tossed
and turned, and tossed some more. He tried counting sheep,
but that didn't help. He lay there, wide awake, listening to
the ticking of the clock. Something's wrong, he thought.
There was something he forgot to do.

"What could it be?" he asked himself. "Did I forget to turn out the light? Did I forget to set the alarm clock? Did I forget to lock the door?"

"Oh no!" cried Ben. "If I didn't lock the door the green monster will get in!"

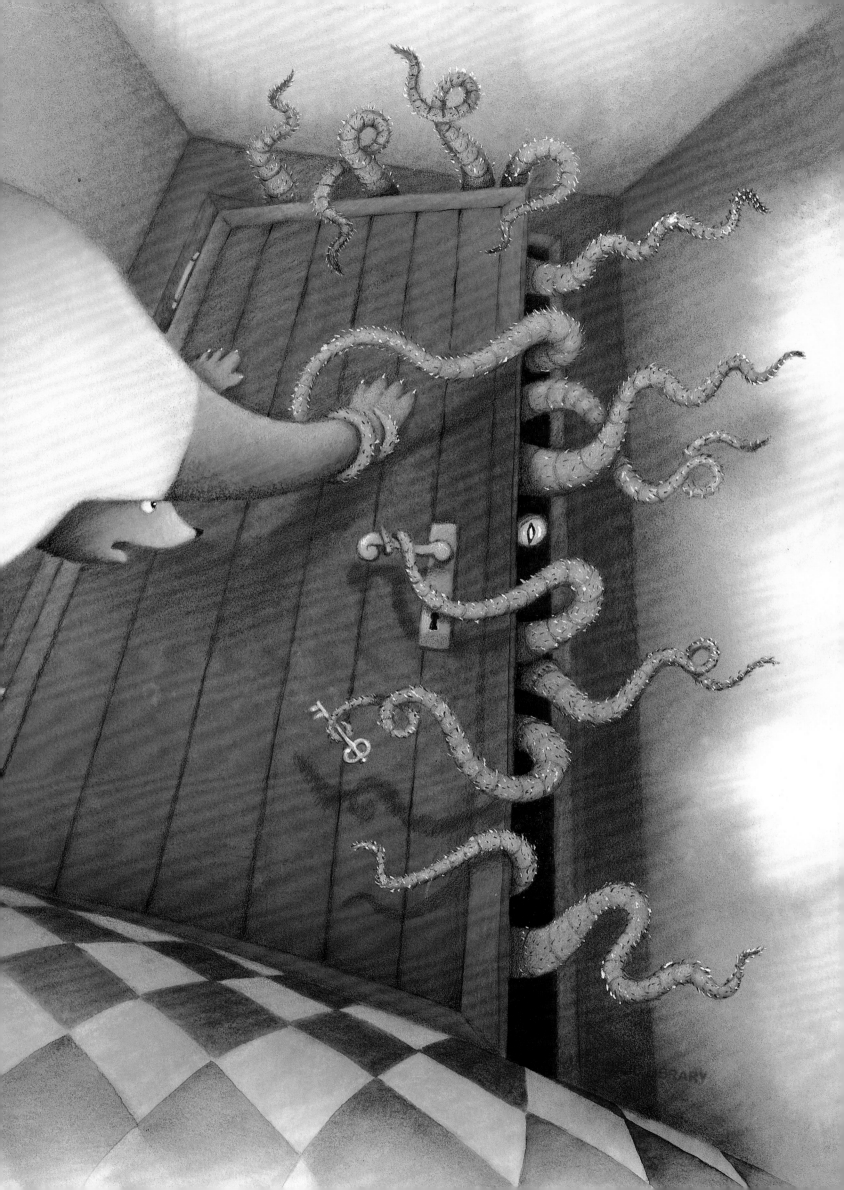

Ben checked the door, once, twice, three times.
The door was locked up tight.

"Whew!" he sighed. "What *did* I forget, then?
Did I forget to feed Luke? Oh no, my poor puppy
must be starving!"

No, Luke's bowl was still full, and he seemed perfectly fine.

"Hmm," mumbled Ben. "Maybe I forgot to water the flowers."

No, the flowers looked fresh and beautiful, not wilting at all.

"What could it be?" Ben wondered. "Did I forget to do the dishes? Did I forget to brush my teeth or wash up before bed? No, I did all those things. What *was* it that I forgot to do?"

Ben Bear took a deep breath. He thought about everything that had happened that day.

We finished painting the doghouse. . . .

We put away all the tools. . . .

We stacked the extra lumber. . . .

"Aha!" cried Ben. He finally remembered!

"Come on, Luke!" he called, hopping on his bike and pedaling away.

Ben stopped at a candy store and knocked on the door. "May I buy some candy?" he asked.

"Sorry, we're closed. Come again tomorrow."

Ben rode on and spotted a girl carrying some flowers.
He called to her. "Please, could I buy your flowers?"

The flower girl was happy to sell the whole bunch to Ben. He hopped back on his bike and raced off. At the end of the street he stopped in front of a small house, walked up to the front door, and rang the bell.

Chris Croc opened the door. "Ben, my dear friend!" he exclaimed. "What are you doing here so late?"

"I couldn't sleep," said Ben. "I forgot something very important."

"What?" asked Chris.

"I forgot to say thank you for helping me build the doghouse. So I'm saying it now: Thank you!"

"Well, you're very welcome," said Chris. "What are best friends for? Come in, come in, let me make you some tea."

The two best friends sat down and enjoyed one of their luscious cakes together.

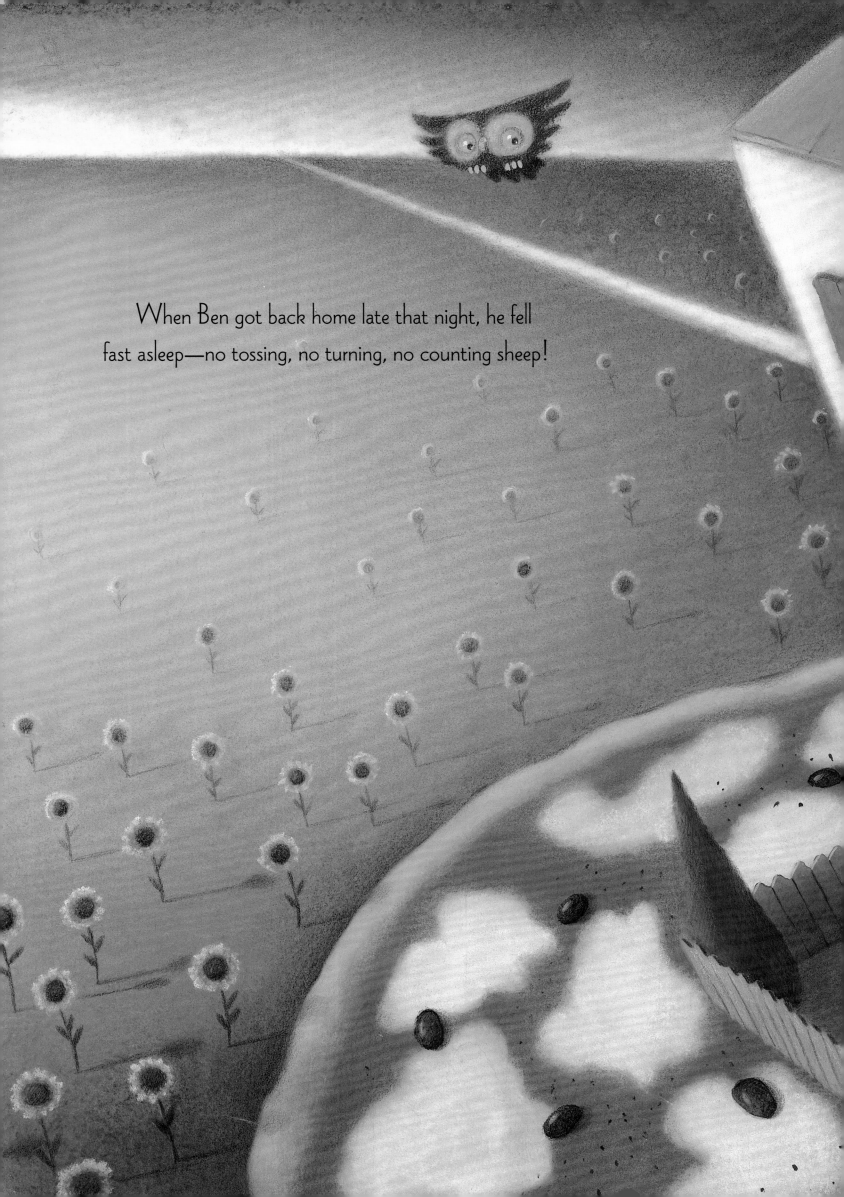

When Ben got back home late that night, he fell fast asleep—no tossing, no turning, no counting sheep!

First published in Taiwan by Grimm Press

First English-language edition published in 2008 by Purple Bear Books Inc., New York

For more information about our books, visit our website: purplebearbooks.com

Library of Congress Cataloging-in-Publication Data is available.

This edition prepared by Cheshire Studio.

Printed in Taiwan

Trade edition

ISBN-10: 1-933327-38-3

ISBN-13: 978-1-933327-38-9

1 3 5 7 9 TE 10 8 6 4 2

Library edition

ISBN-10: 1-933327-39-1

ISBN-13: 978-1-933327-39-6

1 3 5 7 9 LE 10 8 6 4 2